CAN YOU SEE WHAT I SEE?
100 FUN FINDS

READ-AND-SEEK

WALTER WICK

Cartwheel
·B·O·O·K·S·® SCHOLASTIC INC.

New York Toronto London Auckland Sydney
Mexico City New Delhi Hong Kong Buenos Aires

Text copyright © 2009 by Walter Wick.
"See-Through" and "Bump, Bump, Bump!" from *Can You See What I See?* © 2002 by Walter Wick; "Button Fancy," "Games Galore," "Junk Drawer," and "Chock-a-Block" from *Can You See What I See? Cool Collections* © 2004 by Walter Wick; "Such a Clatter!," "Down the Chimney," "Visions of Sugarplums," and "Not a Creature Was Stirring" from *Can You See What I See? The Night Before Christmas* © 2005 by Walter Wick; "Spring Things" from *Can You See What I See? Cool Collections* © 2006 by Walter Wick.

Library of Congress Cataloging-in-Publication Data
Wick, Walter.
    Can you see what I see? : 100 fun finds / Walter Wick.
        p. cm.
    "Beginning reader, level 1, 50-250 words."
    ISBN 0-545-07888-1
    1. Picture puzzles–Juvenile literature. I. Title.
    GV1507.P47W5114 2009
    793.73–dc22

2008019333

ISBN-13: 978-0-545-07888-7
ISBN-10: 0-545-07888-1

10 9 8 7 6 5 4 3 2   9 10 11 12 13/0

Printed in the U.S.A. • First printing, January 2009

Dear Reader,

Read the words and find the hidden objects. For an extra challenge, cover the picture clues at the bottom of each page with your hand.

Have fun!

Walter Wick

Can you see

10 pins,

3 pigs,

and 2 bats?

Can you see

9 birds,

3 cards,

and 2 cats?

Can you see

5 cookie kids

and 3 trees?

Can you see

4 windows,

1 cane,

and 2 skis?

Can you see

2 boats,

2 dogs,

and 1 pail?

Can you see

3 ants,

3 eggs,

and 1 nail?

Can you see

4 horses,

8 checkers

in a box?

Can you see

2 trees

and 5 birds

on blocks?

Can you see

2 spoons,

2 locks,

and 1 key?

Can you see

4 candles,

4 planes,

and 1 Z?

Can you see

2 fish,

2 birds,

and 1 plane?

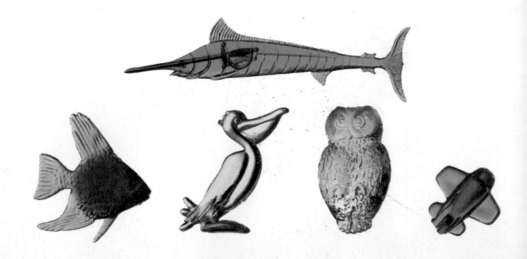

Can you see

3 birds,

3 red wheels

on a train?

ant

bat

bird

block

boat

candles

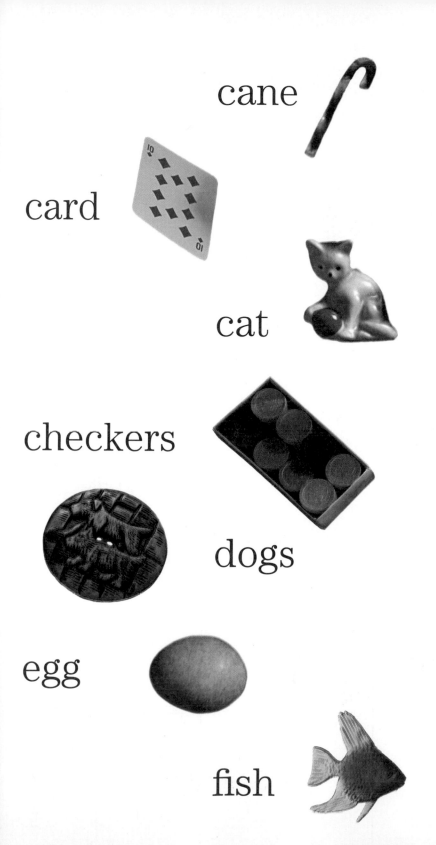

cane

card

cat

checkers

dogs

egg

fish

horse

key

kid

lock

nail

pail

pig

pin

plane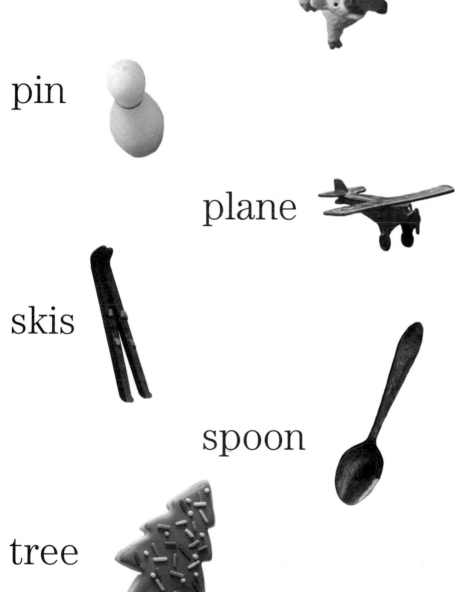

skis

spoon

tree

wheels

window

z